Chartreuse

Christy Beck

Chartreuse

The Balloon Was Green With Envy

By Christy Beck

Chartreuse is a work of fiction. Any references to historical events, real people, or real places are used fictitiously. Other names, characters, places, and events are products of the author's imagination, and any resemblance to actual events or places or persons, living or dead, is entirely coincidental.

No part of this publication may be reproduced, stored in a retrieval system, or transmitted in any form or by any means, electronic, mechanical, photocopying, recording, or otherwise, without written permission of the publisher.

www.Chartreuse2020.com

For Celina and Cierra,
Live fearlessly and proud. You will do great things. I love you.

Christy Beck

TABLE OF CONTENTS

Christy Beck

Prologue

There she was, walking down the street,
singing a little ditty as her heels hit the concrete.
Click, clack, click, clack, her shoes made a loud
smack
as she was walking on the pavement and not
looking back.

It was late, and she was alone
on her way back home.
She'd just left the church, a late revival,
for extra perks, and single survival.
There was a man there watching her,
and she didn't know he was staring and plotting
dirt.

When it was time to go,
he was the first one out the door.
She didn't see him anymore,
so she decided to leave after "Praise the Lord."
That's when she hit the street
and walked quickly down the concrete.

Speeding up as she passed
brick walls and construction land.
It was a huge development on the stop,
and it went as far as two blocks.
She came to an opening, and she could see
a man standing there, smoking some weed.

She did not want to cause alarm,
so she crossed the street to avoid any harm.
The man took notice, and through and through,

he crossed the street and followed for a minute
or two.
There at the end of the site, all open and creepy.
The lady stopped walking because she felt a little
sleepy.
She stopped to take a look at her phone.
She wanted to call an Uber to get a ride the rest
of the way home.

The man came up quick and drew out a gun.
He put it to her face and told her not to scream or
none.
He grabbed her by the waist and pulled her out
of sight,
where he brutally attacked and raped her that
night.
She cried and screamed. She prayed to the
Lord;
this felt like a dream from fright night deployed.
She couldn't believe the evil plight,
because she held up her rosary in plain sight.

The man was swift, quick, and released a little
bit;
that's when she had a plan-
She stabbed him in the eye with her rosary in
hand.
The man screamed and rolled around.
She had time to get off the ground.

She ran as she couldn't fight,
took off her shoes, and took flight.
As fast as she could go

to the fire station, she felt cold.
She was bleeding, and she didn't know.
He ripped her abdomen with every blow.

In the comfort of the authority, she told her
horrific story,
and she swore loyalty
to any man that could catch this fiend and bring
him to glory.
She wanted her revenge
but mostly wanted to get rid of this image.
Because after that day, her internals became so
mean
that the evil man gave her a couple of things…

Christy Beck

Chapter 1

The Birth

Nothing about this pregnancy was normalized.
From the baby's red curly hair to the light green eyes.
Her skin was fair, just like her mother's.
She was a regular baby, just like the others.

She was a cute little thing, should have been a bundle of joy.
But all the mom could think about was the fact that she was not a boy.
She was plagued with preeclampsia and faint morning sickness,
diabetes, high blood pressure, and chills, they were vicious.

When forty-two weeks came, she was well overdue.
The woman was ever so glad that this pregnancy was through.

There was enough to deal with from the rumors
and stares.
Friends and family wanted to know how this
bastard baby would fare.

They were concerned as they ought-
because everyone knew how she fought,
to bear this child, and carry it to term,
even though her pregnancy was a germ.

Dirt and grime are things you can wash away,
but this pregnancy was like a parasite up until
the birthday.
Babies are a blessing, people would say.
You'll eventually learn to love that baby one day.

The day of birth was a very hard one.
She had issues on her mind as heavy as a ton.
She didn't have parents because they passed
when she was five.
But she did have her coworkers that cared if she
was alive.

She sat in the maternity ward with one flower
and one card.
Loneliness and her were always on one accord.
She lived alone in her tiny home and never got
bored,
so it really didn't matter to her now that there
were no visitors.

But what she couldn't get off her mind,

is how the rapist got away and never served
time.
The woman was dressed nicely for the church
singles event.
The man pled in court that the short skirt invited
consent.

Charged as a harlot that drove a desperate man
insane,
the court ruled in favor of the man as they played
a morality game.
They said he was intoxicated and filled up with
drugs,
he went into a church that night looking for some
love.

They pleaded temporary insanity and said he
was a broken man.
They gave him mental therapy and a slap on the
back of the hand.
The woman was sentenced to a lifetime of
shame,
the man's innocence conviction threw dirt on her
name.

Nevertheless, there she was,
holding a baby that needed love.
Needed a house, food, pampers,
And enough clothes to fill a hamper.

Ribbons, bows, and ponytails,
the future of this kid no one could tell.
She was brought to life with an evil fate.

The existence of this child has been terrible up to date.

The woman turned into a Mom, and nothing was the same.
She was nervous, feeling regret, feeling hard to tame.
But the baby is here now and needed a name.
The mom was thinking so hard as if she were playing a chess game.

She knew her child was to be born with a purpose too.
She wanted her child to be a winner but who ever thought of an accident being a winner.
All the woman could think about was the fact that her child was a newborn sinner.

This was forced on this woman, in one stolen night.
That same night she was raped out in plain sight.
That is how this baby came to be,
but at that moment, it felt like a badass dream.

As the woman sat back to think,
She was just sitting there, the nurse in the hospital says, "Um, can you blink?"
Startled. "Oh, my bad, I didn't know how long this would take.
'Cus all I can think about is that this baby is a mistake."

"Oh, don't say that," exclaims the nurse.

"Babies are a blessing, and she's too cute to be
a curse."
The woman has heard that before a thousand
times.
As if thinking the truth was a premeditated crime.

Nevertheless, she had to give this baby a name.
She was serious about it that it almost drove her
insane.
Thinking about it so hard, she felt a little dizzy.
Finally, "Ok, I think I'll call her Missy."

Because of the mistake I made by letting him do
this to me.
Missy is the name. It's short for what it means;
A mistake, a blunder, to err, a travesty.
How could God allow this to happen to me?

I was the most faithful servant under the sun.
I used to go to church every weekend,
sometimes just for fun.
I carried my Bible and rosary everywhere.
I took my communion and confessed with care.

Why did this have to happen to me?
They say bad things always come in a combo of
threes.
What else could possibly go wrong in my life?
Not to mention the fact that I'm nobody's wife.

I have to do this parenting thing all on my own.
I'm still having problems trying to find a home.
Now I have to take an extra life with me,

I don't know if I can do this. It makes me want to scream!"

"You'll figure it out, and It'll be okay, I'm sure," said the nurse confidently as she walked out of the door.
The baby was left in that weary woman's care.
Everyone hoped for the best and wished her well. Don't be scared.

But fear was not the only thing that this woman was feeling.
There was something else brewing hot, boiling to the ceiling.
PTSD is the acronym for this problem.
Her feelings were meek, sad, depressed, and solemn.

The mom would stay in bed; she got up, maybe...
Little to no attention was given to the baby.
The house was a mess and dark as a cave;
this was no way for a mother to behave.

But when it came down to it, she tried to get through it.
She did the best she could, despite the sad violin music.
She was otherwise okay, except on most days when she struggled to keep her brain clear of haze.

It was hard to resist the thoughts of violence that
exists in her brain.
She must be insane,
the unbelievable things, it was mean;
this woman's thoughts and dreams.

She was going crazy.
Her parenting skills were very lazy.
She kept thinking what if this baby disappeared,
no one would miss.
What other better idea to enlist?

How about adoption?
She could possibly live with that option.
In her mind, she'd be alone, what fun.
No more bad dreams, no more shun.

Her entire family treated her negatively.
That had a big effect on her mental stability.
She was doing her best living in a trailer park
home.
But she had voices in her head, and she wanted
them gone.

So she waited until night time, she had an evil
plot.
She wanted to get rid of the baby and make the
voices stop.
She prepared herself, and the baby rolled up in a
blanket;
wrote a note that said *Thanks for taking my kid*.

She took the note, and she fastened it

to the top of the basket.
She packed a bag with food, clothes, and a special treat.
A free baby to a home for anyone they meet.

It didn't matter; she just didn't want to be the one to take on this job, a huge manifestation.
That's when she stopped at the fire station.
Put the baby on the front step with a little hesitation.

Just when she was about to take off and run.
The Fireman came out and said, "Oh, hello, hun.
Don't you remember me?"
The woman had no idea who this could be.

"It was late one night, about a year ago.
You came to the engine house, and you said you were cold.
Well, after that you fainted and passed the hell out.
We found out you were attacked, that's what the cold was about.

You were bleeding so much it gave everyone dread.
For, Miss, we thought you were nearly almost dead.
But we got you to the hospital just in time, though.
I'm glad to see you're okay, didn't think we'd hear from you.

So this is your baby? I'd heard you have given
birth.
Isn't she cute, the most precious thing on earth?
So what are you doing here? What is this about?
I'm glad it wasn't raining. I think we're having a
drought."

The Fireman chuckled and chatted; his smile
was kind.
They talked as if they knew each other for a very
long time.
He showed some concern, and that eased her
mind.
Looking at him, he was handsome, strong, and
fine.

"Let me take you to dinner; it's the least I can do.
A dinner, or a cocktail, for just me and you."
The woman was flattered, and she didn't know
what to think.
She knew that the baby had a dirty diaper, and it
was starting to stink.

"Um, okay, that's fine," she said with a slight
smile.
I've never been on a date, at least not for a
while.
Ever since I got pregnant, I haven't had the time
for me.
But you seem like a nice guy, with the perfect
personality."

She accepted the invite,

and he took her out that night.
She left baby Missy with a babysitter
while they went out for Margaritas and a Mexican
dinner.

It had been a long time since she invited a man
in.
This man brought the light that made the
darkness end.
Encouraged to do better, now her life could
begin.
Ever since that crazy night, he has become this
woman's very special friend.

Chapter 2

The Accident

As baby Missy got older, she didn't like it one bit.
Every time the Fireman came over, she always threw a fit.
He wanted attention, but she needed more, especially when the baby was getting into everything while crawling on the floor.

Baby Missy couldn't have been any more than two.
When she crawled on his lap and took a bite of his food.
He wasn't paying attention when Missy grabbed the toothpick from the rye.
He was eating a sandwich, and the bread was very dry.

Missy's mom was baking biscuits from the can you have to pry.
The Fireman wanted to steal a kiss; he had to sneak it from behind.
He was still holding Baby Missy as he walked across the room.
Suddenly, the can popped open! It sounded like a boom!

 "ARGH!" went the Fireman as he dropped the baby on the floor.
She mistakenly stabbed him in the eye, and he couldn't hold her anymore.
He didn't mean to drop the baby as he quickly grabbed his eye.
When the baby hit the floor, she didn't even cry.

The toothpick went in deep. They tried to pull it out of his head.
When they finally got a grip on it, yanked it out, his whole eyeball was red.
He let out sounds of pain because it went right to his retina.
Drew blood, dripped on the floor, and really scared that poor fella.

He grabbed his face, and he said, "I can't see.
Please pick up the phone and call an ambulance for me."
Missy's mom was ashamed. She thought it was a mistake.
Seeing that much blood was really hard to take.

She had to snap out of it and not focus on the
blood.
The Fireman was rolling on the floor by now, a
sign that wasn't good.
The woman swears it was an accident; she's
sure that it was.
Although, something about Missy's smile
seemed dissonant and smug.

The Fireman went to the hospital when the
ambulance came.
His diagnosis was an eye patch and rest for a
couple of days.
But there was no explanation for why he stayed
away.
He didn't see Missy's mom for a while, and life
was surely gray.

△△△

Fast forward about a year. It's Missy's birthday.
It was scorchingly hot and not humid that day.
Missy is turning four, a celebration to boot!
Mom threw a party with no constellation in
pursuit.

Few friends or family ever show up.
This child was not popular with the other
relatives.
But they came by to visit and see this beautiful
little girl.
Whose eyes were still green most beautiful in the
world.

Someone brought a confetti popper,
it was supposed to be a show stopper.
With confetti and glitter,
it was supposed to be a side-splitter.

There should have been lots of laughter and fun.
It shot off like a loaded handgun.
Which startled little Missy,
and sent her in a tizzy.

She jumped up, and by mistake,
tossed up the whole damn cake!
It was lit with four small fires,
atop the cake, cute decor attire.

The mess was big and out of sight
because pieces of confetti did ignite,
as it fell on everything, in that space-
even the curtains. They were lace.

The curtains were ablaze and quickly spread to
the couch, the table, and all of the food.
The house was destroyed in 600 seconds.
They had a minute to get out of the burning
situation.

At that point, Missy began to live her revelation.
Mistakes were her existence in constant
representation.
Now Mom was convinced her life was a blunder;
She thought, *this baby is the one that put me
asunder.*

She had a child that was cursed in a strange way.
Now they were homeless, where would they stay?
Luckily the Fireman was on duty that day.
He was her hero again, and it must be fate.

He offered to give her a place to stay.
Her and little Missy, they could come in today.
There weren't many options, no time to delay.
So they gathered their belongings and went to his place.

He lived in a neighborhood right on the outskirts of town.
It was nice and quiet with other neighbors around.
The big white house was down the street from the market,
in a sleepy little town with family values in target.

In the middle of town there was City Hall.
They had a *Waffle House* and *Pizza Hut* and a very small shopping mall.
Everyone knows everyone, that's just how it is.
Mostly everyone is related or some kind of distant kin.

Moving in with the Fireman was the best thing to happen thus far.
He gave them shelter, food, and security. She could even borrow his car.

By having a yard and dog right now, things were looking up.
Especially since their trailer was taken in a fire that was very abrupt.

It took some time to settle in because the woman didn't want to impose.
But the Fireman wanted a relationship when he offered her a rose.
Finally, feeling like everything's okay, the mother and daughter had a new life.
Feelings of bliss had remained for a while, no more strife.

They lived together for about a year, and everything was just fine.
Just the three of them together, all of the time.
Constantly growing as a couple and family then,
"Beep, Beep," honked the moving truck. New neighbors are moving in.

Chapter 3

Moving Day Friend

It was a family just like theirs,
aside from the skin color, they were much less fair.
Other people couldn't help it but to stop and stare.
Treating them differently really wasn't fair.

All had skin, brown, and golden
as if they were toasted by the sun and chosen
to represent the world in this small town.
They've never had anyone with the color brown.

Missy had never seen any black people before.
She'd only heard about the struggle and color wars.
Although in town there was one little kid,
but he was something else, something like Mexican.

Missy took it upon herself one day,

to go next door to ask the little girl to play.
When she went to the door and rang the bell,
they were taking too long, so she started to yell.

Knock, knock- "Hello? Anyone present?"
The door opened up, and the people were
hesitant.
She saw the father first as he came out and said,
"hi."
He was a tall black man; he looked like a nice
guy.

When his daughter came to the door, she looked
outside.
She was feeling kind of nervous, so she started
to hide.
Missy was quick thinking and pulled out some
candy,
she offered a piece to prove her philanthropy.

"What's your name? I'm Missy Lane, and I live
on the block.
I like your green dress. Where'd you get this
frock?
Green is my absolute favorite color too.
Did you know the color is created by mixing
yellow and blue?"

The little girl smiled, she said, "Thanks, my name
is Aleena Green.
I like green too, so I know what you mean.
When I grow up, I want to be a fashionista or
singer."

She made a big twirl holding up one pinky finger.

"With dance moves like those, I'm sure you'll be
seen.
 Which is why from now on, I'm calling you Lima
Bean!
Or Lima Lena Beana, it's all the same.
If you want to be a singer, that could be your
stage name."

Both girls had a laugh, they thought it was funny.
They also commented on how green is the color
of money.
They talked for a while about this and that.
Until it was dark, and Missy had to go back.

For the entire summer, every day, they decided
to play.
Missy and Aleena would run around in the yard
for most of the day.
When the girls would skip together, holding
hands, just in case,
people would look rudely upon them turning up
their faces.

The Old-fashioned folks were not used to this
new edition.
 Watching them with hateful eyes hoping for
eviction.
They did not like the Green's because of their
skin.
Some often said mean things and made fun of
them.

Of course, the girls attended the same school in town.
There was only one grade school and one high school close around.
There came a time when Missy had to defend her best friend from a bully when they were nothing but 10.

The bully at school couldn't keep his hands to himself.
He pulled Aleena's hair and tugged it hard as hell.
He said, "It must be nice to feel nappy and happy.
With hair like that, you need to be sad and sappy."

"Leave her alone!" shouts Missy from the rear.
"I really don't like bullies. I will bite you, like Tyson bit that ear."
Just then, Missy pushed the bully's head with her finger.
And the Bully threw a fist quickly he did not linger.

Unfortunately, when the Bully threw a punch with his fist,
Missy moved right in time for the Bully to miss.
Instead, he hit the pillar in the middle of the cafeteria.
He broke his knuckles in two places, which caused instant hysteria.

"Get away from me, you trash; you deserve each other.
White trash and black dirt; my uncle calls you nigger lovers."
Missy made a face that sent chills down his spine.
Something about Missy's threats was really scary this time.

Missy was the toughest girl in school anyway.
But something in those green eyes made the Bully stay away.
From that day on, people were warned not to mess
with Aleena while in school, show respect, and nothing less.

One day when the girls were playing with a green ball;
it bounced over a fence- one that was wooden and tall.
Into the yard of an old white man;
he wasn't nice anyway and blacks, he wasn't a fan.

He would sit on his front porch and told everyone to stay off his land.
He was always using obscenities and waving his hands.
He was the tall and thin type, with a slightly hunched spine.

It was hard not to notice he was outside most of the time.

But this time, he was gone for the moment.
After a powerful kick, the green ball went soaring.
Their ball bounced high into his territory.
His yard was forbidden- it had a house with one story.

"I'll go get it," Aleena stopped to say.
"I'll be really quick, don't worry. It'll be okay."
"Wait," said Missy, "I know what to do.
Here, take this rosary. Jesus will protect you.

That man is evil, and you need all protection.
I don't want anything to happen to you," said Missy with affection.
Aleena took the rosary without much thought.
Besides, she could use it to pray just in case she got caught.

"My mom gave this to me after a terrible fire.
She told me it would protect me against evil inspired."
Aleena took the necklace, not sure what it meant.
But she trusted her friend, and it was a nice sentiment.

She disappeared behind the fence almost way too long.

When she came back, Missy knew something
was very wrong.
Aleena was visibly shaken and upset.
She knew Mr. Mean had something to do with it.

"What happened?" Missy asked. "What took you
so long?
What happened to our ball? Please tell me
what's wrong?"
Aleena just stood there and stared into space.
She said, "That man is terrible," with a look of
disgust on her face.

"What happened? Where's our ball?
You're dirty, did you fall?"
"Yes, on the way out I tripped and fell;
I was running fast as hell.

When I first walked in, I saw an overgrown yard.
It had tall corn stalks and a pumpkin patch with
vines that were very hard.
I walked around, and I thought I saw our ball by
the board.
It turns out it was a green fruit, something like a
gourd.

Finally, I saw our ball; it bounced into the shed.
I went inside and looked around, feeling a little
dread.
I saw some tools and magazines that were full of
pretty ladies.
The only thing about the pictures was everyone
was in their panties.

I knew it was only a matter of time before Mr.
Mean came back.
But when I turned around to leave, I heard the
storm door slap.
I ducked my head and started to run back
towards the gate.
That's when I looked down at my hands and saw
that I took the magazine by mistake.

I tried to hurry back to the shed all the way
across the yard."
"You left the ball and took the book? That's the
dumbest thing I ever heard."
"I know right; I was just so afraid,
just then he was coming my way, his privacy I
did invade."

"Okay, so what happened next?
I just know he was mad and vexed."
"I was getting closer. I thought I was free,
but I tripped on a vine and fell to my knees.

From the ground, I looked up,
and there he was standing in the buff.
He was naked, and I could see
his private parts waving at me."

Then Missy got angry, that wasn't right.
She got angry enough, and she wanted to fight.
But instead, Aleena already knew what to do.
Go tell her parents; tell them the whole truth.

The girls ran to find Aleena's mom.
She was washing dishes in the kitchen with the radio on.
Aleena was crying and apologized to her mom, sincerely
She thought her mom would be mad and made her eyes look teary.

Aleena's mom was concerned about what Dad would do.
Because, man to man, showing your privates is the worst thing to do.
When Dad got the word, he was shocked and highly disgusted.
He went down to the precinct because he wanted him busted.

The police came and issued a warrant.
The old man would be forever labeled as a child deterrent.
His privacy and rights, he now had to surrender, because, after that day, he was labeled as a sex offender.

Mr. Mean was embarrassed; he really couldn't take it.
The scrutiny he received about him being naked.
In his own yard, what an unfair conviction.
He was highly upset with Aleena, let's not fail to mention.

He swore he would try to get back at her some day.

If he had to be labeled, he planned to make her
"pay."
He wasn't really sure of what he would do.
But he wished he could intimidate and scare the
whole crew.

While he was plotting and scheming and being a
tool,
Missy and Aleena had to go back to school.
They lived each day, getting better as friends,
promising to be there for each other until the very
end.

They went everywhere together, sleepovers,
what more.
All the girly things that girls like to explore.
Missy and Aleena best friends- partners in crime.
Spending lots of time together all of the time.

Aleena was a better person because of Missy
too.
She was much more relaxed with actions
subdued.
Missy swore havoc on anyone
that comes in between her and her best friend,
the first and only one.

ΔΔΔ

One day, Missy was excited and could hardly
wait.
She'd been at school all day, since about early
eight.
Waiting for the bell to ring at three,

seemed to take forever, time was slowly
creeping.

She wanted to take Aleena to a babbling brook.
Which went to the river pass overlook.
They could take some photos on top of the
bridge,
for 'kicks' and selfies- social media images.

At the sound of the school bell, of course, Aleena
agrees
to take the long way home to venture into a new
scene.
Whether it was the scenic route or a new
expedition.
She trusted her friend; she was full of new
inventions.

Plus, Aleena hadn't really explored her new town
yet.
Especially after all the drama in it.
So going as planned, they set off on their
destination.
Skipping and singing with no hesitation.

But just as expected, something terrible was in
hindsight.
Because Missy's the child born with troubles and
mistakes, forthright.
They had no idea the pain that was in-store.
Which brings us to the cataclysm that starts in
chapter four.

Chapter 4

"D" Day

Missy was always jaunty and wayward.
Trying to control her behavior seemed like hard labor.
Perhaps because she was bold and brave as one.
The things Missy did, she did it for fun.

She didn't really mean to cause harm or be bad.
She probably inherited a little mischievousness from her dad.
It wasn't apparent until after some occasions when she got caught in the moment of alarming situations.

She was usually pretty good and stayed out of trouble for the most of it.
But this one time, her boasting was idiosyncratic.
Here they were walking down a wooded path, taking pictures, and posting them on *Instagram*.

At first, it was quiet, and there wasn't anyone
else.
They kept walking and singing, and they thought
they were by themselves.
"Look up ahead, a bridge overlooking a rushing
stream."
Missy said to Aleena, "Think of all the good
angles and things.

Come on, take my picture as I walk across the
ledger."
As dangerous as it was, Aleena thought and
knew better.
Standing on the bridge, the stream turned into a
river.
The wind picked up, and the spray gave the girls
a quiver.

Unfortunately, the girls failed to see a car
approaching.
It was Mr. Mean. He was driving slowly...
coasting.
From afar, he noticed their innocent little fun.
He waited for the right moment to be an evil one.

Suddenly he hit the gas.
He was approaching the girls really fast.
His best opportunity to be somewhat vicious,
honk the horn and fire spitball ammunition.

As he sped fast...
That spitball had the perfect path.
It hit poor Aleena in the face,

she backed up and pushed Missy by mistake.

Aleena wiped her face; it made her scream and
yell.
When she realized her reactions is why poor
Missy fell.
She looked over the side of the bridge.
Missy was still hanging on to the ledge.

"Help me, best friend. Please, I don't want to
die!"
 Aleena reached for her friend, just out of reach,
she tried.
She stretched out her hand and said, "Grab me!
Come on!"
But the only thing she could save was Missy
green ribbon.

Screaming and SPLASH! Missy fell into the river.
The stress of this moment made Aleena's whole
body shiver.
Missy could not be seen in the water.
And Aleena couldn't swim, so jumping in she
didn't bother.

What could she do? Her friend was gone.
Missy couldn't possibly swim or hold her breath
for that long.
Aleena knew what to do. She stopped to call her
father
to report the tragedy of Missy falling in the water.

The police tried their best, as much as they could.
Locating the body did not turn up so good.
It seemed like forever, as long as it took.
When the carcass was found it had a deteriorated look.

The body was badly battered and torn up a bit.
So the only choice for a burial was to cremate it.
Golden shiny metal- it was a tiny little urn.
It was the only option after the body had been burned.

ΔΔΔ

Two weeks later, the funeral begins.
The chapel was empty, and there were hardly any friends.
Just a few acquaintances that came to pay their respects.
The funeral and the people there were as sad as they can get.

Especially Aleena, who cried in the back pew.
Overcome with so much grief, her parents didn't know what to do.
She sat and listened to the pastor as he recited his words.
Was angered and annoyed that he didn't know much about this little girl.

After the funeral, the urn was given to Missy's mom to take home.
But after having it for a night, she wanted it gone.

The stress of realizing her only child was in it,
was too depressing and sent her anxiety to the
limit.

The next day,
Missy's mom begged for the funeral director to
give her daughter a grave.
Although it was after the fact,
unfortunately, what was missing was money to
pay for that.

The funeral director figured it too,
but he said he would see what he could do.
He hired his nephews to work for free.
But the price of doing a good job is hard to
receive.

They only dug a little bit.
They figured the ashes would only sit.
It should have been a six-foot-hole.
But they figured it didn't matter, who would
know?

After shallow digging - only a tiny pit.
They dumped the ashes inside of it.
They covered it up and stole the urn,
with very little effort or concern.

Missy was dead,
and there was nothing else to be said.
Specifically, the bourgeoisie people
showed little concern instead.

Balderdash in the mist,
it doesn't make very much sense;
strange things started happening
and it started with a visit twist.

Chapter 5

The Balloon

Aleena's whole family was from the hood.
They were an honest family that was doing pretty good.
The mother was a teacher carrying side jobs of whatever.
The father worked in law enforcement as a policeman officer.

They came from a town close to Chicago.
When the father got a new job, it was time to go.
He'd gotten a promotion and honors on the force.
They asked him to spread his expertise and start a new course.

He was required to pack up his whole family.
Move to a rural agrarian type of liege.
He swore his loyalty to his newfound challenge,
to be a newfound hero- some kind of gallant.

They needed a new detective.
Someone that could make their town more
effective.
A strong and intelligent man.
They wanted someone with a plan.

The father was gracious; he had no idea what
would happen if he and his family made this
jump.
So on moving day, they came with a bunch of
surmises,
most of the people didn't like their kind, Oh, what
a surprise...

Even with their important positions,
racism veered its ugly head with many
submissions.
Victims are rarely ever at fault,
trouble comes looking for innocent people when
evil is sought.

Their first day in town, the family went to the
store.
They received many stares and scrutiny galore.
Waiting in line, just like anyone would
proved to be hard when others were not good.

An older white lady with blonde hair and blue
eyes,
wore a yellow church dress with a big handbag
on the side.
She was in the store behind the family with one
item.

She had little patience for blacks; she absolutely despised them.

The lady clearly saw them standing, but she pretended not to notice.
She pushed into poor Aleena, cut the line as if she were Mr. POTUS.
The family tried to take a small stance,
but received no apology, only a mean, merciless glance.

That was the same day, while bringing in grocery bags,
they saw a little white girl with a green sucker in her hands.
She was playing in her yard that was not very far.
The truth is Aleena was curious too but did not dare leave the exterior.

Especially after what happened earlier at the grocer that day,
it seemed like having friends in this town was on serious delay.
Almost spoken too soon with solidarity premonitions,
there was a knock on their door, inviting many inhibitions.

Hearts were beating fast as the father went to the door.
He knew he could not run forever; he couldn't take it anymore.

He grabbed his pistol and slowly went to see
who could be knocking? Who wanted this family
of three?

He opened the door, and who did they see?
A little girl there smiling and looking pristine.
"Hi. Hello," she said.
While raising her head.

She was holding a green sucker,
her lips were all puckered.
And that was the day,
she introduced herself as Missy and asked
Aleena out to play.

From that day, it was apparent,
a new friend they both would inherit.
No more anxiety and moving woes,
they both could claim she is someone that I
know.

As they began to play together,
they became birds of the same feather.
Even though their skin tones were different,
their friendship was magnificent.

Everything was perfect. Life was looking great.
Which brings this story up to date.
That terrible day and that terrible deed,
when that old man's car was driving up the
street.

His actions caused a reaction, that's a scientific
fact.
His actions were the cause that threw Missy
back.
When she fell into the river and died on impact,
violence and vengeance soon comes to
payback.

ΔΔΔ

After the repass, it was time to visit the grave.
So Aleena's mom agreed to take her to visit that
day.
She searched the graveyard looking for the
tombstone.
Mom didn't want to get out of the car, and she
had to do it alone.

Paying her last respects at Missy's burial plot,
Aleena was alone, but she was talking a lot.
With her, she brought a few things to reminisce.
It was the deceased birthday when Aleena came
to visit.

Aleena was talking to the tombstone for a little
bit,
Missy's rosary and ribbon, she put on top of it.
Aleena's just sitting remembering the good
times.
I can't believe she's gone; a horrible revelation.

Just as she's about to start her own private
ceremony,

she hears her mom on the phone telling
someone the whole story.
"Yesterday was the funeral, and now we're at the
cemetery.
I'm so glad my daughter is such a good girl and
really caring."

Aleena's mom is upset; she's sad for her child.
She knew visiting the graveyard would take a
little while.
But as much as she wanted her daughter's heart
to heal from this scorn…
She was ready to go and loudly honked the horn.

BEEP! "Let's go! It's been like an hour!
I'm ready to go home; I need to take a shower!"
With the honk of the horn and small unnoticeable
detail,
it is important, at most, of how the rosary
accidentally fell.

Aleena was startled; at first, she hadn't noticed it.
The rosary fell down and toppled a little bit.
It landed on the hollow ground with a small, tiny
thud.
It was turned upside down, and that really wasn't
good.

Aleena must be swift because mom was aching.
Time to leave this creepy place where a lot of
lives were taken.
Out from her pocket, she took out a green
balloon.

She wanted to finish her ceremony, but she had
to do it soon.

So she stood on the grave and said an
incantation.
She had no idea the meaning of this heartfelt
intonation.
She was full of love and desperate for arise,
as she said these words with tears in her eyes…

"Ashes to ashes, dust to dust. Ashes to ashes,
dust to dust."
Then she drew back a huge breath and blew in a
huge gust.
She knew she was leaving soon,
so she grabbed up the ribbon and the rosary. It
was hard to consume.

She didn't notice the balloon…

Miraculously, however, the balloon was floating.
Almost to the point where it seemed to be doting.
Attached to Aleena, the only one,
who created this monster, a menacing one.

For whatever reason, no one knows
how Missy's spirit was forced in with one blow.
Which was probably the reason that it can float.
No one ever questioned it, though.

Not even Aleena. She was a clever girl;
but young she was and living in a fantasy world.
It never dawned on her that after sealing it,

in order to float, you need to put in helium!

Aleena just took out the ribbon that belonged to
the slain,
she tied to the end of the balloon so it wouldn't
fly away.
When she got to the car and sat in the back seat,
mom was still on the phone describing the feat.

"My child is so brave; she's truly a godsend.
Move to a new town, deal with racism, and now
losing a best friend.
I don't think I could do it, I hope now her soul is
at peace.
Maybe I can help her. Provide her with therapy at
least."

Insanity and apparitions correlate synonymously.
Aleena was a sad girl right now obviously.
Apparently, at that moment, it was difficult not to
hear,
the balloon made a familiar sound, like
whispering in Aleena's ear.

"LeeeeeNaaaaaa!" A raspy voice made a tiny
little sound.
Aleena took a deep breath and looked all
around.
She could hear Missy's voice, to her wild
bewilderment.
She thought she was going crazy and started to
vent.

"Mom! I think Missy's here…
It's almost like I can hear her in my ears.
Mom! Are you listening? I think I feel sick.
Mom look at my balloon, that's it! I think she's
inside of it!"

But her mom was still on the phone,
as they were driving on a two-lane road.
Ignored the cries of a serious tone
because in that car, she thought they were
alone.

"MOM! Look and believe!
Please pay attention to me!
This balloon is my friend. I know I'm not crazy!
Look at it now, stop being so damn lazy!"

With that accusation, the mom got annoyed.
Whatever Aleena was talking about, Mom could
not avoid.
She turned around with a snap
and tried to look back into the back seat at
Aleena with a balloon in her lap.

Still holding the phone, she didn't notice
the car swerved and veered, turning for a
moment.
They crossed over to the other side of the road,
another car swerved and spent to avoid a
devastating blow.

"Oh, no!" Screech! A halting stop- quick on a
dime.

"I hope no one got hurt; we turned just in the nick
of time."
Looking up and around and checking the scene.
Mom cut off the devious fiend, Mr. Mean.

When he gathered himself and noticed it was
"those blacks!"
He got even madder, and he had his rifle in the
back.
He got out of the car to calculate the damage
thus far,
he started yelling and screaming at Aleena's
mom in the car.

She got out of the car and tried to calm Mr.
Mean.
But the more she explained, the more he started
to scream.
"You'll pay for this, you bitch! Hope you know this
is strike two!"
I'll shoot out your tires... You know what?! That's
what I will do."

Mr. Mean started to walk back to the trunk of his
car.
He popped it open, removed the gun, and left the
trunk ajar.
Aleena was hurt, she'd smacked her cheek
against the glass.
The balloon was boiling as if being filled up with
hot gas.

'Cus the next moment of decree...

The balloon took off and took flight
independently!
It flew out of the open car window.
It disappeared into the sky; where it went, no one
knows.

There were still many cars passing by with
constriction.
 Looking at the dissolution, solemn tuition.
Just then, like a terrible ironic premonition,
the balloon appeared in oncoming traffic right
into somebody's line of vision.

Chapter 6

Blind spot

Screeccccchhh! BOOM! Is all that they heard.
Then they saw Mr. Mean lying lifeless on the curb.
He was struck hard to the point he was bleeding from his nose.
Struck so hard to the point that it was his time to go.

He was dead on impact, and everyone knew,
a man of that age surely wouldn't pull through.
It was an accident, of course,
although weird discourse.

How this came to a head,
and Mr. Mean ends up dead?
Standing in the street, Aleena's mom couldn't believe this feat.
Looking at that old man lying on the concrete.

She ran over to check and see
if the old man was still breathing.
She started to panic and screamed for help.
Luckily on the road, she was not by herself.

People all over started to gather,
they didn't notice the balloon rather.
They tried to help the old man,
as the balloon floated back to Aleena's open
hand.

She created this monster and released an evil
incarnation.
Brought the balloon to life with independent
animation.
She didn't know the vengeance that Missy swore
on everyone;
especially those that were abrasive or mean to
her loved ones.

Even in death, Missy swore to protect her.
Swore inexplicable pain, death, or torture.
Coercion from an object that should be
inanimate,
but this balloon could float around purposefully
independent.

But no one else could see the poltergeist
thralling.
Initially, not at first, Aleena was in the backseat
bawling.
All this manifestation for Aleena's well being.

How did the balloon leave and come back
without anyone seeing?

Death number one, or should be called number
two.
This would have never happened if Mr. Mean
wasn't in pursuit.
He was the sole reason for Missy's tragic death.
But she got her revenge in a fatal traffic accident.

Although, payback's a bitch, and karma wins
again;
evil begets evil and leaves blood on hands.
Negative attitudes increased all over the land.
The town's people developed attitudes because
of circumstance.

"It must be those niggers! They are followed by
destruction it figures,"
said a buzz around town. "The black people must
be the triggers!"
Gossip from the citizens made the horrific scene
worse.
But life had to go on, despite this negative
discourse.

The father had a job to do, no sitting around.
He conducted investigations and ignored the
town.
His job just got harder, to tell the truth.
He couldn't ignore the ill-treatment from people
uncouth.

The faithful stayed loyal as loyal can get.
Especially Missy's mom and the Fireman betwixt.
They were white in a town with no family around,
so they decided to stick with the people that were
brown.

Archaic as it may sound,
it was a small country town.
But the Greens were determined and decided to
stay.
The blind spot was racism, like Hell to pay.

Even in this day,
racism paves the way
for evil to come alive, making demons strive
and ruin some lives.

Chapter 7

The Church

Aleena's mom said, "The only place I know
where refugees are a truce,
we need to go to the church where dissolution is
much loose.
Give thanks, praise God, forgive the situations.
Open our hearts and our minds to glory
presentations."

Sashaying in church all in their Sunday best.
Everyone's watching and whispering, contrition
adlibs coming abreast.
Trying not to disturb anyone.
Shoulders back, eyes straight, only talk to some.

This was a Catholic church, quiet as a mouse.
The alter boy just entered and received
communion in his mouth.
The priest said, "Come one, come all, receive
His greatness, last call.

Jesus gave his life to everyone, come get your
blessings, come get some."

Just as a lady was about to receive,
Aleena had her balloon in between her knees.
The lady was rude; she pretended not to see
as she shuffled past and forcefully bumped their
seat.

The balloon floated up and flew in the way.
It somehow flew right in that lady's face.
The lady decided that's she's had it with them.
This was the same blonde lady from the grocery
store incident.

This time she was sure and highly offended.
That balloon was in the way and had to be
ended.
She walked back to the altar, looking for the
perfect satire.
She decided she would "accidentally" push the
balloon into the fire.

The candles in the Catholic church were tall and
always lit.
The balloon could touch the heat unintentionally
and ruin it.
The noise would be loud and distracting, but no
one would assume,
that she was the person that popped the balloon.

Standing in line, going down to the front.
Positioning herself to pull off this evil stunt.

It was their turn to receive wine from the priest.
At that moment, her plan she needed to
complete.

The balloon was haunted, but no one knew;
Until Aleena's hand was tugged, and the balloon
flew-
Out of her hand and just missed the priest.
He stumbled and threw the wine goblet to his
feet.

The lady was shocked by the sudden emission.
The balloon was floating around like a
Ghostbuster apparition.
"Grab the balloon! Don't let it get away."
While frantically grabbing someone bumped into
the stage.

All of the wine was dumped out…not some.
The wine was spilled and starting to run.
The candles were knocked over and began to
ignite
the high alcohol content that was fueling the fire.

Everyone ran out of the church that was engulfed
in flames.
The fire spread quickly, probably because the
wood was stained.
Oiled and waxed figures- it was a beautiful old
church.
Now it was burned up and crumbled in a huge
pile of dirt.

The blonde lady swore to get her revenge.
She visited that church ever since she was a kid.
The woman was swift, "Do you know what you
did?"
She picked up a stone and threw it at the kid!
It barely missed Aleena's head.

It hit the balloon instead…
It didn't pop or bounce back,
Aleena had to try hard to keep it under wraps.

The lady was confident that she caused an
unsettlement in the bunch.
She said to the priest son, "Come on, let's go
have lunch."
The family was sad and mystified,
while crocodile tears swelled in their eyes.

They couldn't believe this church travesty.
Not to mention, the blonde woman was really
mean.
Encountered her for the second time,
but this time she was obvious with her slime.

"Come on, family, let us go.
I know a place to eat located up the road.
Let's get away from this bafflement,
and get some brunch for the kid."

Just as they started to walk away,
the balloon did something very strange.
It waxed and waned a little bit,
with a gust of wind it flew intrepid.

Blown in the wind, away from the friend.
It did not fly very far; it did have an end.
It ended up floating beside the blonde woman
who,
despised and hated the existence of the balloon.

She jerked her head right; she could see in her
side vision.
Standing in the store front, there was nothing but
her reflection.
"Hmm," she thought as she carried on her
traipse,
she could have sworn she'd seen a balloon on
the side of her face.

The balloon was ominously floating in an alley up
ahead.
The way it was floating would have caused
anyone dread.
"Oooh a balloon," says the boy yelling from afar.
He went for it and gave chase with all his heart.

He ran for the balloon that got closer to an
escape ladder.
The boy climbed, no hesitation, to get what he's
after.
The blonde lady takes notice and comes from
the rear,
she didn't notice, however, that the balloon stuck
in the gear.

When the boy pulled the balloon to get it free,

the escape ladder lever was pulled with the
string.
It came down quickly, and the lady was in the
way.
It came down heavy and impelled her in the face.

Of course, being hit in the head,
the lady was dead…
The ladder was to blame, or maybe the balloon,
all the same.
Yet again, here is another mistake, caused by
Missy Lane. That's her name…

Chapter 8

Schoolboy John

As it turns out, the lady that died
was the priest's wife, and she despised
any other person of color.
Especially her husband's son and his real
mother.

The boy was not Caucasian; he was half white
and Mexican.
When he was only two, he was adopted and
given to them.
The illegitimate son of the pastor, couldn't deny
his paternity, everyone knew.
Because it was obvious that he was sleeping
with the beauty from the lawn crew.

Waywardness to his marriage,
it caused some disparage.
Infidelity led to this little boy,
and now this lady was employed.

Drudgery is the worst
and felt like some kind of curse.
But with due process of the wind,
she accepted him as her own kin.

△△△

The boy's name is John.
After the escape ladder accident- his stepmother
was now gone.
He felt responsible for her death.
The details of her passing he kept thinking to
himself.

After she was taken away in the ambulance,
he sat in a chair, holding his head in his hands.
He was holding the balloon by the string
when he heard a sound in his ear that started to
ring.

"Hey, John, over here."
It sounded like his old friend Missy in his ear.
He thought he heard her voice, but how?
He must be really tripping now.

He stood there, gaping at the green balloon.
He must be hallucinating. He felt like a buffoon.
Inside the balloon, it was getting dark and
cloudy.
Then he was sure he heard a little girl's voice
loudly.

"Hey John, over here!
I'm talking to you. Can't you hear?"

This time he heard it again,
but it was Aleena, his schoolmate friend.

"John!" she said, "you have my balloon.
Where'd you find it? I'm glad I caught up with you soon.
I need it; I must have it; it's special to me.
It always floats away, then returns. I bet that's hard to believe?"

"I'm not sure, and I don't know why,
but I think I heard a faint tiny cry.
It was calling me or something, at best, I tried.
I think it had something to do with why my stepmother died."

"Your stepmother is dead?"
It's crazy how death spreads.
It seems like ever since this balloon was erected,
there's always been something happening unexpected."

What do you mean?" asked John as his eyes got wide.
He hoped that she was someone in which he could confide.
He wanted some enlightenment from this crazy event.
Another reason for this terrible incident.

He listened to Aleena without hesitation,
as she explained the whole unfortunate crazy situation.

As Aleena explained she started to realize,
that she really liked the color of this young man's
eyes.

He was handsome and smart, and his attitude
was fair.
He smelled of cologne and had a part in his hair.
Unpretentious as he was, the best type of guy,
he was popular and humble and kept positivity
high.

But evil is vindictive, especially one captured in
plastic.
It got angrier anytime someone would pass it.
That poltergeist inside did not like other people.
New friends to Aleena was totally unacceptable.

A couple of days later, when John began to
mend;
he really liked Aleena and wanted her to be more
than a friend.
Taking pictures and posting them was becoming
a trend.
That's when the balloon took notice and plotted
her revenge.

Missy's envious spirit seemed to boil inside of
that balloon,
every time John came over, daily after school!
He was getting too close to Aleena, and she was
starting to forget
about her old best friend, the green balloon, with
the ghost inside of it.

Aleena and John could be found walking around
town.
It was really hard to hold a balloon too, so she
had to put it down.
The balloon was left plenty of times sitting in her
room.
It wasn't a problem because Aleena was happy,
no impending doom.

Her parents were not home one day when he
came by.
She snuck him into her room; she thought she
was being sly.
But Aleena was young, almost too young to
know
that boys with Adam's apples are quickly too
grown.

They went to her room and closed the door.
They sat on her bed, and he started touching her
more.
He was trying to kiss her, and he was doing too
much!
Aleena started to squeal after too much lust.

"Stop John; I thought we were best friends.
I'm not ready for a boyfriend, and I don't want to
pretend."
"I like you, Aleena. Don't you like me? Let me
kiss your lips and then you'll see
how easy it is for me to slip between those
knees."

Aleena was scared because she really didn't know
that he liked her like that. He tried to take off her clothes.
She arose from the bed, went to the bathroom, and locked the door.
She shouted from behind, "You really have to go; my parents will be home at four!"

She looked in the mirror and scolded herself aloud.
"I thought he was my friend, and I just wanted to be apart of the crowd.
I wish I never asked him to come up. How did I get into this mess?
I must put him out and protect my innocence."

John was patient. He was doing just fine.
He decided to just sit back and give her some time.
She would eventually come out from behind the door.
He assured her he didn't want to kiss her anymore.

Instead, he just laid in her bed feeling played.
While looking around her room, his frustration stayed.
He sees the balloon. He hits it like a punching bag.
Then a strange thing happened, which really made him mad.

The balloon didn't move; it took the punch like a
champ.
There was no recoil, bounce, or any moving
amps.
It seemed like the balloon was on a guided
course.
Because somehow, the balloon had an
unbelievable force.

It slowly hovered forward
in John's direction it moved toward.
No coercion. No wind. No breeze.
John began to tremble in his knees.

He saw the face of the evil one.
Suddenly the balloon made an arduous lunge!
It pushed him back irrevocably,
just as Aleena opened the door... Everything
she'd seen.

John had fallen from the second story, and he
was badly hurt
When he rolled off the roof and hit nothing but
dirt.
The great fall that he had as he hit the ground,
seemed to have made a thundering sound.

Chapter 9

The Fireman

It was hot that day, and the lawn needed some care.
So the Fireman was outside in his yard's posterior.
It was a regular day, or so it seemed,
he was off work today and decided to clean.

Just as he was taking out the trash,
he noticed a young man walking pass fast.
He was on his way to visit a girl,
obviously with a flower and a tight curl.

"Oh, hey John, how are you?
It's a nice day, what are you finna do?"
John just answered with a smirk,
"I'm going to Aleena's house, her parents are at work."

The Fireman was busy; he didn't think much

of the young man's plight and mission corrupt.
The young man seemed genuine too,
he was old enough to know what to do.

The Fireman stood and had a flashback to the
time of the church fire.
John wanted to assist; for help he was for hire.
The fireman gave him a hose to help out the
crew.
It was as if this boy was a natural, he knew what
to do!

△△△

The Fireman went on to minding his business,
but as soon as John was gone, he suddenly felt
hesitant.
*I think I should check on my neighbors the
Greens,
because they are not home, and a visitor has
been seen.*

As soon as he had this thought, he heard a loud
THUMP!
He looked over there and saw a body lying in a
slump.
"OH MY GOD! Oh no. I wonder if they know."
He rushed next door and nobody was home.

He searched all around, from top to ground.
No one was at home, and no one could be
found.
So the Fireman ran around the house to assist
the body on the ground.

He called for help and waited for the ambulance sound.

"John, are you okay? Please stay with us!
You're going to be fine, in me you can trust."
Luckily, he wasn't dead. He only hit his head.
Went to the hospital with stitches and a broken leg.

Aleena didn't know, she was on the go.
'Cus she finally figured out that the balloon had an evil ghost.
A spirit oddity and no one believed,
the balloon was possessed and nobody could see.

She walked all day, trying to remember.
Then she thought of that day that was close to November.
Thinking of that odd cold day,
when she went to visit her best friend at the cemetery.

She was taken aback by a thought- very scary.
I need to retrace my steps, and I must hurry.
So she went back to her best friend's grave.
To possibly retrace her steps of what happened that day.

It had been just about a year since Missy's wake.
The quiet, empty church was hard to intake.
She searched for the tombstone and the exact same spot.

She tried hard to remember her words but some
she had forgot.

She looked around the area for any clues to
uncover.
But she didn't find anything that could explain
why the balloon can hover.
Everything looked almost the same,
except for a huge crack that divided Missy's
name.

Aleena looked around for any more damage.
All the other tombstones remained untouched
with plots that were very well managed. The lack
of care given to this grave brought a tear to her
eye.
She lowered her head, and when she looked up,
she could see the shadow of a guy.

He was tall and dressed in red,
with horns on his head.
He was muscular looking and bulky.
Aleena bent down to get a better look low-key.

Who it was, she couldn't see him,
but it looked like a red demon.
Maybe *Tales from the Crypt* can explain,
why zombies and ghouls were the first things on
her brain.

He was standing at the edge of the cemetery.
He wasn't doing anything but standing and
staring.

Aleena wasn't sure of what she should do.
So she gathered her belongings to look for an alternate route.

She began to walk in the opposite direction.
She wanted to get away from that peculiar section.
Her walking turned into a sprint; she was really scared.
Especially when she turned around, and nobody was there.

Aleena stopped running and looked around this foggy place.
She made a full turn and then there he was standing in her face!
"Gasp!" said Aleena as she bumped into the Fireman.
He was standing over on top of her, holding out his hand.

"I thought I'd find you here, I feared for your safety.
I'm glad my search for you wasn't very long and lengthy.
I saw you praying, and I didn't want to interrupt.
So I stood by and waited, I hope that time was enough.

I saw what happened to John at your house.
Then you disappeared all of a sudden, what's that all about?
This red suit that I wear helps me to save lives.

You can trust me Aleena, in me you can confide.

What happened, sweetheart? Tell me the truth.
Don't leave out any details, I think I can help
you."
"I don't know. I'm not sure. It was a complete
accident.
I don't know what happened. It seemed like an
attack!"

"An attack?! From who?
No one was there, just you.
I came and looked. I was right there.
I checked the whole house and the exterior.

Which seems confusing for you to say an attack.
Tell the truth, Lena. Who pushed John back?
When he fell from your room and space,
I looked at the window and saw your face."

Aleena tried to explain how the balloon came
alive.
It sounded hard to believe, it sounded like a lie.
"So if the balloon is the problem, why not get rid
of it?
This balloon sounds like a lot of trouble, kid."

"I can't. She's my friend.
I love her to the end.
But as soon as things change,
that's when my troubles begin.

But you're absolutely right.

I must end this fright.
I don't know how. It seems impossible.
This balloon is indestructible.

I need to consult an expert on this matter.
Stop the balloon, stop evil, or the latter."
"You need someone with pious priority,"
said the Fireman, "to make evil cease.

I know someone, a Gypsy man.
He can probably help you stop evil plans.
He used to be a traveling shaman, for real.
I think you should go talk to him. He's the real
deal.

He's located on Main Street on the edge of town.
You have to go now I hear the police siren
sounds.
When you get downtown, try to avoid the
precinct.
Take a right pass the bakery and old skate rink.

Go to him now before the police come around.
It will take you some time to get to the edge of
town.
Is there somewhere you can take or put the
balloon;
in order to watch it? So it doesn't know or
assume?"

"I'm afraid to leave it alone,
I don't want things to happen while I'm gone."
"I'll take it to my house to give you some time.

Don't worry. Be swift. Everything's gonna be just
fine."

Aleena agrees, and starts off on her journey.
She needed to do some research, and do it in a
hurry.
It was time to end this. End this insanity.
So she followed her GPS walking coordinates to
see the Shaman Gypsy.

Aleena was worried as anticipation grew.
Who knew what he would tell her, who knew
what she had to do.
But she visited the Gypsy anyway,
to get her horoscope, or whatever he had to say.

She came to a tiny building on the edge of town.
It was small with one window and brick all
around.
She entered the building and looked at the floor,
up to the ceiling there were trinkets galore.

She surely wasn't sure, not even a little bit.
Especially when a tiny old man
came from the back and said...
"I've been expecting you, please sit."

Chapter 10

Shaman Gypsy Talisman

"You've been expecting me?
How can that be?
This is the first time I've seen you and come to meet,"
said Aleena as she went to take a seat.

The gypsy was swift and was known to spy.
He told the young lady, "Well, I can not lie.
I've heard about you and your whole family.
I knew when you moved in; a small family of three.
And your presence caused a disturbance in our quaint little town.
I'm sure you know why; because your skin color is brown.
Some people were not ready for a change like this.

Then deaths increased, and it started with you,
kid."

"We didn't mean to bother anyone; we were sent.
Because my dad is a detective in law
enforcement.
And trust me, I'm sorry to come to you now,
but I need your help to do something. I hope you
know how.

It all started, I think, after the death of Missy.
I visited her grave and gave a private ceremony.
I prayed to God and said rest in peace.
I said some earnest words in holy territory.

It would have been her 13th birthday that day.
That's why on November 13th, I visited her
grave.
She wasn't perfect, but she was my best friend.
We swore loyalty to each other, and I let her
down in the end.

So on her birthday, I decided to do it, not just for
me.
I thought this would help me through it, and give
my broken heart some ease.
I took a deep breath and blew into a balloon.
I tied up the end so it wouldn't float around the
room..."

"Stop, I've heard enough of this somber story.
Now let me tell you where you fucked up and
opened purgatory.

First off, you went to her grave on her thirteenth
birthday.
As I remember it too, that was a Friday...
because in my mind, it always replays.

I was just driving across town, minding my own
business.
When suddenly, something terrible flew into my
vision.
I'm not sure what it was… I thought it was just
latex.
I tried to explain to the fuzz, right after the
accident.

Humph! Get with it, little chick!
The graveyard is full of demons and ghostly
spirits.
You're sitting here claiming your holy story.
Did you really think poltergeists were not in that
territory?

Only the good get to rest in peace.
Did you really think that evil can not be released?
Or maybe you thought her soul wouldn't arise.
Why do you think people say *good morning* after
someone dies?

When you're alive, you have a choice,
in death, you have no voice.
So if you live with good intentions,
your spirit will rise with no suspensions.

But if you live with shame and shun,

the spirit will continue seeking vengeance.
It only seems proper to roam the earth,
in search of proving yourself and unholy worth."

"I guess I never thought of it that way…
But when Missy died, why did <u>she</u> stay?
I was her best friend, I loved her to death."
"Perhaps that love statement is what kept her abreast...

Do you have anything of hers? Something personal and dear?"
"Yes! I have her rosary; I always keep it near.
She gave it to me about three years ago.
She told me it would protect me, so I always kept it close."

"Okay, anything else? Do you have something that she loves,"
asked the Gypsy man as he flips through a book.
"I've kept her ribbon on sight.
I got it from her that very last night."

"Whatever do you mean?"
asked the Gypsy. He was a little worried now, it seems.
"I hold it every day...I mean…
it's tied to my balloon, our favorite color green."

"So now I get it. It must be true.
This town's calamities are all because of you."
"Me! How can that be?

I'm a good girl, check my records. I'm totally pristine!"

"Not by you totally, per se,
but because of the love you gave an evil heart at the grave.
Her love for you truly never dies.
The only way to rid yourself is through your own demise.

If she can't protect you and make good of her promise,
then maybe she'll die, and her soul will be abolished.
Either way, it's up to you to stop this kid.
All the death around you is because of what you did.

So go on now and reverse this intonation.
May Heaven or Hell find destitute revelation."
The Gypsy man was right... *I started this shit.
Now it's up to me to get rid of all of it.*

ΔΔΔ

Aleena walked out of the store, feeling a little better.
She made sure to pick up some talisman and lucky feathers.
She figured a few extra charms wouldn't hurt in this need.
If she had to kill a ghost, lucky charms weren't hard to believe.

She really wasn't sure of what she should do.
She needed to be quick because the longer
apart, the angrier the balloon grew.
It was tied up tightly to the ledge.
It was in the Fireman's house on the stairwell
edge.

Missy's mom entered all depressed and not
herself.
She was still dealing with the tragic death, and
she really needed help.
Her daughter's life was taken so soon, and her
beating heart would not ease.
The mother cried so much about it that it brought
her to her knees.

She couldn't take it; she was just about done.
She decided to leave for fresh air and an
afternoon run.
Not long thereafter, she left,
the balloon was the only witness to a damsel in
distress.

The Fireman was on the phone.
He thought he was all alone.
There was a female voice on the other end.
Sounding very sultry and whispering to him.

"Well hello, Fireman Joe,
Can I come over and play with your big hose?"
Said a soft voice on the other side of the phone.
It was another woman when mom was not home!

That was the last straw the spirit has had it!
'Cus, this was the biggest form of blatant
disrespect.
Mom didn't deserve this; she was just caught in a
mood.
And now was not the time to treat her so rude.

Instead of love, care and sympathy a bit;
The Fireman looked like he had another
relationship.
Furious and hot, the balloon began to move.
It floated independently across the whole room.

It went straight to the back of the Fireman's
head.
It startled him. He was shocked by the proximity
closeness.
"I thought I tied you up over there.
How'd you get over here back in the rear?

What's up with this silly ass balloon?"
It floated to the ceiling, so he went to get a
broom.
But when he came back around,
the balloon was sitting on the floor. *Now it's close
to the ground?*

This was the path that the balloon independently
chose.
He didn't notice the ribbon was tangled up in the
knob of the gas stove.
When the Fireman pulled and yanked on the orb,
the knob was spent, and gas was implored.

It was simply only a matter of time.
Sooner than later, the sound of the doorbell chimed.
It was a lady. She came through the back.
She got close to the Fireman looking really suspect.

While he was holding the balloon, she came in with ease.
She started kissing him, and the balloon he released.
He didn't try to stop her, in full submission.
That was all the evidence needed for guilt confession.

"Wait... Hold on... My girlfriend is gone.
She went out running, and I don't know when she'll be back home.
Let me make you a drink. Just relax a little.
I'll help you ease your mind; come in and get settled."

"Well, okay," said the woman. "Do you mind if I smoke?
I know you're a Fireman, that was a little joke."
But as soon as she fired up and started to take a toke,
the fire mixed with gas and started to explode!

The whole house was blown up, obliteration to a piece.

The fire was so great that anyone around was deceased.
What more can be done? Guess who the Fireman was among...
The other person dead was also Aleena's mom.

Chapter 11

BFF

As one could suspect,
right before the death that a policeman and
fireman, yes, they were best friends.
Just like birds of a feather, like peanut butter and
jelly together.
The girls had a tight bond, and so did their
elders.

The parents hung out on weekends.
They did things together just as friends.
They got as close as a family can get.
When stress was apparent, together, they took a
sip.

Missy's mom needed love from family or friends
(anyone).
And this particular family was different but had a
kid with them.
They had more in common than their differences.

They all moved in town with negative
speculations.

Missy's mom received scrutiny because of the
rape.
Then all those tragedies seemed too much to
take.
Being black in a white town, most people would
not dare.
But at least they had friends that liked them
there.

Unfortunately, after Missy died the two families
tried
to go on with their friendship, but nothing felt the
same inside.
Missy's mom was often sad and then got really
mad.
Losing her only child is the worst feeling she ever
had.

This is probably the reason
that during this hurt season,
that those two had a fling.
It was a normal thing…

-It came after liquor,
It makes emotions come thicker.
Inhibitions are weak
and makes infidelity peak.

They were emotional wrecks,
and one thing led to the next.

Stopped in a halt, completely embarrassed,
because they were careless.

The balloon was present that unfaithful day.
The day the house blew up, the balloon narrowly
escaped.
It was weird how it happened, and it didn't make
sense.
Missy's mom didn't have anything to do with it in
her self- defense.

The police concluded it was the gas.
They couldn't figure out how it blew up so fast.
But as you can guess, it wasn't fun
for the lead detective to detect the death of his
own loved one.

At first, he didn't know, he could hardly tell the
race.
Not even after looking hard at the burnt woman's
face.
It took another second for him to realize,
then hot tears began to well up and form in his
eyes.

It must be when he looked down at the person's
ring finger.
She was wearing a wedding band, one he'll
always remember.
"This is my wife! My best friend and confidant."
Tears rolled down his cheek, and sorrow spread
nonstop.

"How am I going to tell Lena that her mother is dead?"
We just buried her best friend; this is a blow to the head."
The clouds rolled in, it was starting to rain.
"I must go and find Lena to report that her mother was slain."

He rode off looking for his daughter, he didn't know where.
He called her cell phone several times with no answer there.
The town wasn't big, and help wasn't good.
There weren't many people interested in helping a black detective.

ΔΔΔ

Meanwhile, Aleena was on her way back home.
She saw the destruction and picked up her phone.
27 missed calls, all from her dad.
Her phone was on silent while she was talking with the Gypsy man.

Ring….ring... "Hello? Dad, where are you? What happened over there?"
"Lena! Go into the house, I'm coming. I'll be right there!"
She obeyed the command and hung up the phone.
"MOM?" she looked around, but no one was home.

Just as Lena was on her way to her room,
she caught a glimpse of the T.V. it was playing
the News.
It talked about another tragic day.
Just one too many deaths, all in a weird way.

But this time it was much sadder and worse,
the anchorman said it involved a Fireman and
black woman's corpse.
The fire that was ablazed, everyone was
amazed.
The time it took to burn up should have
happened in days.

Aleena just watched the news and sank to the
floor.
With that information, she couldn't take it
anymore.
It felt like a nightmare or some curse from Hell.
She was filled with emotion and started to yell.

Heavily breathing and mad, she knew what to
do.
This balloon's ultimate demise was currently due.
She would do it alone; she didn't need a crew.
But how to do it? She had absolutely no clue.

Chapter 12

Backtrack

*T**he Gypsy man said, if I want to get ahead*
and come from the dead,
then I better get out of bed and use my head.
It's my fault. I am the reason for all this mayhem
and disaster.
How it all started, it really doesn't matter.

All I know is I'm feeling all alone.
I want the people I love to come back home.
Then it suddenly occurs to me,
I haven't seen my balloon in about an hour or
three.

"Where are you? You silly ass balloon.
I know I better get ahold of you soon.
I thought I saw you in the room, but the T.V.
caught my attention.
Well, I'm dead set now on completing this
mission.

There's too many dead too.
All because of what, a green balloon?
Tell me, Missy... when will you be through?
THE ANSWER'S TONIGHT BECAUSE I'VE
HAD IT WITH YOU!

TONIGHT IS THE NIGHT! THIS HAS TO END!"
Then CLAP goes the thunder, which was
followed by strong winds.
It was really raining now, could have been a
Category 3.
The lightning and thunder was the last thing
Aleena needs.

But Aleena couldn't wait much longer.
Somehow she could feel the spirit getting
stronger.
She searched the whole house and came to the
door of the attic.
It was a big red house, three levels, the interior
design was romantic.

The higher you go up, the scarier it seemed.
But as soon as Aleena looked up, she saw the
ribbon tantalizing.
It slid through the cracks; no one could see,
the doorknob made a snap with the turn of the
key.

Aleena tried, and she tried,
the balloon must be inside.
But the knob was stuck and did not budge.

The balloon must be aware of Aleena's grudge.

Just as she stopped to think and think.
Like Winnie the Pooh trying to get in the honey tree.
She knew what she had to do.
Climb out the window on level two.

She could climb up the big oak tree next to the house.
Climb into the attic just like a boss.
Just as she stepped onto the shingles.
The heavy rains made her bare skin tingle.

Oh no, there's Dad, before I tell him what this is all about,
I better do this quick before the real truth comes out.
The dad pulled up quickly, and to his surprise.
Aleena was on the roof, and he couldn't believe his eyes.

He was about to say something as he looked up to level three
when Missy's mom returned home and started to scream.
She had no idea the carnage and the extreme gore.
She screamed even louder and dropped to the floor.

She saw Aleena's dad and asked, "Where is everyone at?"

He just shook his head and said, "I'm
sorry...they're dead."
She already guessed they were dead,
it just sounded better coming from a friend.

Chapter 13

All Fall Down

The rain was coming down hard to the ground.
The thunder kept booming like a loud drumming sound.
When Aleena looked out the window from the third floor.
She could she Missy's mom losing her mind even more.

She was crying and upset. She was all torn up.
There were too many deaths around, and they all seemed abrupt.
Aleena was sorry when she began to realize the truth.
Which solidified the steps of what she had to do.

The window was open when she entered the cove,
but as soon as she entered, COO! There flew out a dove.

Oh, it was just a flying white rat.
I learned in school that they are called fruit bats.

But that wasn't the only thing to be scared of.
Evil was present with no signs of love.
"Come on, Missy, come out I know it's you.
Come on out, Missy, it's time to face the truth."

Slowly the balloon emerged lit up by the moon.
It hovered stoically silent in the middle of the
room.
Just then, Aleena's dad opened the door,
and the balloon flew out the open window with a
train-like roar.

It flew out so fast because of the breeze,
it flew out of the window and got stuck in the
tree.
"No!" Aleena shouted, "this was my chance.
I've got to get that balloon, this is my last
advance."

"What are you talking about, my little one?
We have each other... Mom's gone…"
"I know that is why I must put a stop to this."
Missy's evil poltergeist has made Aleena
vindictive.

She pushed her father away and ran
to get to the open window as fast as she can.
She didn't even stop to think,
all she knew was she must get up that tree.

Dad yelled at her, "Lena! Don't do it! Just let it go,"
But what Aleena's dad failed to know
is the balloon was the problem
and it really had to go.

She was in the tree now looking up.
In a tree limb, the ribbon had gotten stuck.
Aleena kept looking higher to avoid looking at the ground.
When she looked up, she could see the balloon twirling around.

I can not believe this shit! Is this going to be it?
Or is this another one of the balloon's evil tricks?
Just seems a little dumb after all that damage,
getting stuck in a tree is a little ironic.

The closer she got, she could definitely implore
that the balloon was really stuck and couldn't fly anymore.
Aleena was brave; she didn't waste a second.
She climbed the tall oak tree that was woody and relentless.

Climb as she might, with absolutely no regard.
The higher she got, she began to pray to the Lord.
Heaven help me; this is not a good look.
Please open the gates if my young life is took.

Down on the ground, she heard a big fit.

People were gathering around to witness all of
this.
They knew she loved her balloon, but was it
really worth the risk?
Somebody pulled out their phone and began
recording this.

The girl and her balloon entangled in a tree.
It was a terrifying spectacle; the whole
neighborhood came out to see.
She was scooching across the branch, and a
little closer is all she needs...
Then "OH, NO!" Aleena slips and is hanging like
a trapeze.

Gripping as hard as she could;
she had two hands wrapped around the wood.
When she tried to pull up, the balloon tried to
break free.
It pulled really hard on the limb of the tree.

This looked like a deja vu disaster!
And it nearly was considered one after the
actions thereafter.
Crack! The branch started breaking, an
inevitable bough.
She was hanging on for dear life and screaming
down to the crowd.

"Help me, somebody!
I can't hold on much more!"
Snap! The bough breaks,
and she falls down to ground floor.

△△△

Even to this day,
nobody could say,
why Aleena Green decided to climb up the tree
that way.
They were just glad that she was okay.

The hospital is where she awoke the next day.
When she opened her eyes, God had answered
her prayers.
She was surrounded by the people that she
loved the most.
They were looking at her as if they had seen a
ghost.

Her dad and Missy's mom all had a sigh of relief.
Even schoolboy John was there smiling happily.
"Dad, what happened? I thought I was dead."
"Well, dear, you fell from high up and bumped
your head.

That was the scariest moment of my life to see
you in that tree.
Just tell me one thing... why a climbing spree?
That was crazy young lady. What on earth were
you thinking?
What if you had... Oh, never mind, I'm just happy
you're blinking."

"I've got a present for you."
"You do?
What is it?

Now I'm kinda happy you came to visit."

Surrounded by loved ones with tears in their
eyes.
Some of them were nurses and friends that
started to laugh and cry.
Aleena wanted to know that evil had an end.
Just as she was about to question that, she
turned and saw her old friend.

It was the green balloon. By the light of the
moon,
Dad went up to free it last night from its tree limb
cocoon.
"I know how much you love this balloon, it was
the reason why
you went up in that tree in the first place and
climbed up so damn high."

Aleena's dad seemed happy as he gave her the
balloon back.
She hugged him and thanked him for keeping on
track.
Just as Aleena was about to sit back and relax,
a slow, sneaky smile appeared just like the
Cheshire cat.

When they were all feeling relieved, and their
hearts began to swoon,
that's when Aleena says, "Hey, can I borrow your
pencil?" And she POPPED the balloon.
She laughed, they all gasped, the confusion they
couldn't pass.

But the evil spirit lives on as transparent gas.

ISBN: 978-0-578-62503-4